A Stack of Alpacas

MATT COSGROVE

For Madeleine and John
My niece and nephew
(who are nothing at all like Reece, Roo and Drew)
— M.C.

First published in 2019 by Koala Books
An imprint of Scholastic Australia Pty Limited

First published in the UK in 2020 by Scholastic Children's Books
Euston House, 24 Eversholt Street
London, NW1 1DB
A division of Scholastic Ltd
www.scholastic.co.uk

London ~ New York ~ Toronto ~ Sydney ~ Auckland
Mexico City ~ New Delhi ~ Hong Kong

Text and illustrations copyright © Matt Cosgrove 2019

ISBN 978 1407 19933 7

1 3 5 7 9 10 8 6 4 2

The moral rights of Matt Cosgrove have been asserted.

Papers used by Scholastic Children's Books are made from wood grown in sustainable forests.

Typeset in Mr Dodo featuring Festivo LC.

This guy is called **Macca.**

He's an alpaca!

He collects **funny caps,**

And **loves**
to take
NAPS!

That guy is called **Drew.**

He's Macca's nephew!

He's round as a **bubble** and . . .

Here are Macca's nieces. He loves them to pieces.

They're called
Reece and **Roo**,

And they're trouble **TIMES TWO!**

'STACKS ON Uncle Mac!'

CRACK!

'Oh, my back!'

When the gang came to stay, they played up all day,
And thought it was cool to break every rule.

RULES
- eat your veggies
- play nicely
- use your manners
- be tidy
- act sensibly

They **flicked** all their peas
And **scoffed** down lollies.

They **fought** over toys

And made lots of **noise.**

VROOM!

BOOM!

There was **SMASHING** and *splashing!*

FIGHTING and biting!

Binging...

...then **whingeing.**

Macca looked at the mess
And **CRACKED**
from the stress!

'**Reece, Roo** and **Drew**
I expect more from you!'

Seeing Uncle Mac
completely **blow his stack**,
The trio were surprised ...

After they **cuddled**, the alpacas all **huddled**,
And came up with a plan to get things
spick and **span**.

From high to low

It was **go!**

Go!

Go!

Reece **rubbed** and **wiped.**

Roo **scrubbed** and **swiped.**

Drew **dusted** and **scooped...**

Until they were all **POOPED!**

'**I'm so proud of you three,**'
Macca whispered softly.

But as he left them to sleep,
He accidentally went . . .